Dear Parents and Educators,

Welcome to Penguin Young Readers! As parents and educators, you know that each child develops at their own pace—in terms of speech, critical thinking, and, of course, reading. Penguin Young Readers recognizes this fact. As a result, each Penguin Young Readers book is assigned a traditional easy-to-read level (1–4) as well as an F&P Text Level (A–P). Both of these systems will help you choose the right book for your child. Please refer to the back of each book for specific leveling information. Penguin Young Readers features esteemed authors and illustrators, stories about favorite characters, fascinating nonfiction, and more!

Llama Llama™: Llama Llama Talent Show	LEVEL 3
	F&P TEXT LEVEL J

This book is perfect for a **Transitional Reader** who:
• can read multisyllable and compound words;
• can read words with prefixes and suffixes;
• is able to identify story elements (beginning, middle, end, plot, setting, characters, problem, solution); and
• can understand different points of view.

Here are some **activities** you can do during and after reading this book:
• Summarize: Work with the child to write a short summary about what happened in the story. What happened in the beginning? What happened in the middle? What happened at the end?
• Problem and Solution: Work with the child to go through the book and identify the following elements from the story. What was the main problem the characters faced? How did they work to fix the problem? What was the solution they found?

Remember, sharing the love of reading with a child is the best gift you can give!

*This book has been officially leveled by using the F&P Text Level Gradient™ leveling system.

PENGUIN YOUNG READERS

An Imprint of Penguin Random House LLC, New York

Penguin supports copyright. Copyright fuels creativity, encourages diverse voices, promotes free speech, and creates a vibrant culture. Thank you for buying an authorized edition of this book and for complying with copyright laws by not reproducing, scanning, or distributing any part of it in any form without permission. You are supporting writers and allowing Penguin to continue to publish books for every reader.

Copyright © Anna E. Dewdney Literary Trust. Copyright © 2021 Genius Brands International, Inc. Published by Penguin Young Readers, an imprint of Penguin Random House LLC, New York. Manufactured in China.

Visit us online at www.penguinrandomhouse.com.

ISBN 9780593224731 (pbk)   10 9 8 7 6 5 4 3 2 1
ISBN 9780593224724 (hc)   10 9 8 7 6 5 4 3 2 1

llama llama
talent show

based on the bestselling children's book series
by Anna Dewdney

Llama Llama is at school.

His teacher, Zelda Zebra,

shares fun news with the class.

Tonight there will be
a talent show.

Kids and parents
will perform together.

Gilroy quacks
like a duck.
Llama Llama
and his friends laugh.
"It's one of my many
talents," Gilroy says.

Zelda Zebra smiles.

"You see, we all have

hidden gifts," she says.

Outside, the kids find

their parents.

They tell them all about

the talent show.

Nelly asks
Llama Llama
what his talent
will be.
Llama does not
know yet!

Llama Llama and Mama Llama
go home.

They try to think of a talent.

They could dance.

Or jump rope.

They try a

sock-puppet show.

They try a balancing act.

They try shadow puppets.

Nothing feels right.

"This isn't working,"

Llama Llama says.

"Nothing is.

What are we going to choose?"

Mama Llama is not worried.

She knows they will find a talent

that they both like.

"I have an idea,"

Mama Llama says.

"Let's go for a walk.

It will help us think more clearly."

Llama Llama thinks

that is a great idea.

He sees Luna, Nelly, and Euclid

working on their talents.

Llama Llama is ready

to get back to work.

He and

Mama Llama

try a magic trick.

 Llama tries
to make Mama
disappear.

It does not work.

He tries to pull Fuzzy out of a hat.

It does not work.

Llama Llama
starts to worry.
They are
running out
of time.

If they do not choose an act soon,

they will not have time

to practice!

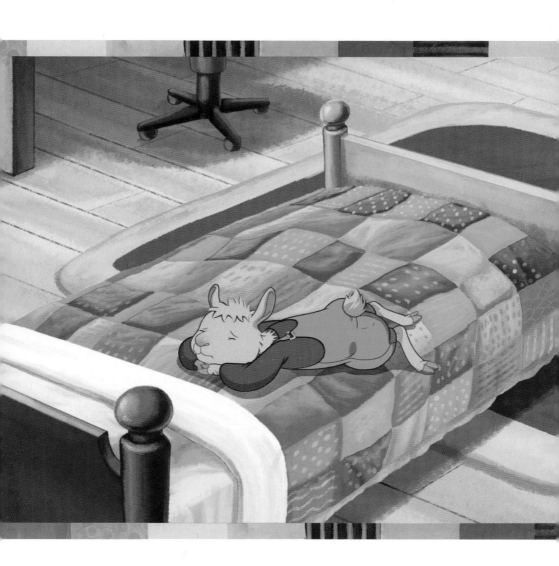

21

Mama understands how

Llama Llama is feeling.

Making choices can be hard.

But Mama has an idea!

"You're fun and funny,"
she says.
"And you and I
like to do a lot of
fun and funny things."

Mama shows Llama Llama

a flower that squirts water.

"Our act could be

an old kind of comedy

called vaudeville," she says.

Mama Llama explains
that vaudeville is a mix
of singing, dancing,
and clowning around.
Llama Llama loves that idea!

Soon it is time for the talent show.

Euclid and his dad

fly a toy plane.

Luna and her mom

make a chain of paper giraffes.

Nelly and her parents
do a balancing act.
Gilroy and his mom
bounce soccer balls
on their knees.

Finally it is Llama Llama's turn.

He and Mama

ride bikes backward.

They play kazoos.

They even do a magic trick.

As they leave the stage,

Mama slips on a banana peel.

Everyone claps.

Their act was fun and silly.

"That was so fun!"

Llama Llama says.

His friends agree.

Everyone did great!

31

"Thanks for making
our act our own, Mama,"
Llama Llama says
as they ride home.
Mama smiles.
"I loved it, little Llama."